RASPUTIN'S CLOAK OF DARKNESS
BOOK ONE
BY BOBBY F. BROOKS

Archaeologist Dr. Rasputin (Razz) Freeman was on his way to the city of Cairo in Egypt for a meeting with a well-known professor of archaeology. During his trip, he stopped off in a small village to rest and get something to eat. As he wandered through a local market, he was approached by a young boy wanted to sell an ancient scroll, which the intrigued doctor bought after some haggling. When he discovered the secrets on the scroll, his life would be changed forever. He witnessed murders and human sacrifices. From the moment he held the artifact, he decisions Dr. Razz Freeman made could change the course of human history

.

TABLE OF CONTENTS

Contents

CHAPTER 1.

THE SCROLL

What should I do now? This is going to be a big decision;
it could mean the difference between life and death—my
life or death!

Just a few weeks ago, I was traveling through Egypt, on
my way towards Cairo, across parts of the Sahara desert.
I had been searching for ancient Egyptian artifacts. I've
been following leads for years. Yes, I had found some
treasure here and there, but nothing very significant until
an ancient Egyptian scroll.

I was traveling through a small village, in search of food,
and was approached by a young boy, around 16 years old.
He asked me if I was a treasure hunter. I told him I was
an archaeologist, almost the same thing, but I only looked
for old things.

"What's your name?"

"Dr. Razz Freeman"

The boy told me he had found a scroll, and he would be
willing to sell it to me for a price. Of course, my initial
thought was that it must be a fake scroll, because there
are so many of them around. I told him I was not
interested. He was persistent, proclaiming the papyrus was
ancient. I became more curious and inquired how much he
wanted.

"How much will you give?" he challenged.

I pointed out I hadn't seen the scroll yet, but offered him five US dollars, and was met with cries that it was worth far more.

"How can I give you a price on something I haven't even seen? You must bring it here for me to look at."

"It is not safe to bring it here!" the boy cried "Someone might take it from me, and then what would I have? A safe place is not far. Come, I will show you."

I knew this would probably be a mistake, but I relented, voicing my concerns that I might be cheated. The boy shook his head, beckoning me. "I will not cheat you, that is not my way. We can be there in a little while." I followed him out of the small village, toward the cliffs behind it.

We walked for about 30 minutes when I said to him. "I thought you said it would only take a little while."

"Just a little further" he said, "we're almost there." We continued on. After another 30 minutes we reached a small clearing. "It is here," the boy announced.

I looked all around but I didn't see anything. Noticing my confusion, the boy pointed to a shrub off to the right, and walked over to move the shrub to the side. Behind it was a small entrance to a cave.

"You first." The boy got down on his hands and knees ready to crawl in. I handed him a flashlight. "You might need this."

He started crawling through the opening, and I followed close behind him. We crawled about 10 feet before the tunnel opened up into a larger chamber. It was plenty big enough to stand up in. The boy turned to his right, where another small tunnel was just visible in the dim light. He began to crawl through that one as well and I followed once more. This time we moved about 20 feet before it opened up. The tunnel appeared to be carved out by hand. The boy pointed to what appeared to be a niche in the wall. "It's in here. I will get it for you."

My interest piqued. I couldn't figure out why he would go to this much trouble just to sell me a cheap fake scroll. My doubts were indeed dashed, because what the boy brought out was a real, genuine papyrus scroll. He said he found it weeks ago, but there was no one here in the village that he could sell it to, until I came along. I asked him how he knew it was a treasure map.

"Whether it's a treasure map or not, it is still worth money." He was right. I knew that no matter what, the scroll was worth at least several thousand dollars. I could see that it was Egyptian from the hieroglyphs on the edges.

The boy broke into my thoughts with a small cough. "How much will you give? The money you pay me will buy food for my family and once it is gone I will have nothing else."

That statement made me have second thoughts about offering him $10 or $20 for the scroll that he knew very little about. Once more, I asked him to name his price.

"Would you pay me as much as $100?"

"That's a lot of money." I said.

"Okay," he said, "then give me $75, and I will be happy and my family will be happy." Attempting to lighten the mood, I asked him if he took credit cards. His eyes dropped and his lip began to tremble.

"I'm just kidding!" I clarified, not wanting to upset him more. "I'll pay you the cash." The boy's face lit up again with a smile. "On one condition. You must not tell anyone that you sold this to me. Is that a deal?"

"Oh yes," said the boy, "it's a deal." I put the scroll in my carry bag and crawled back out of the cave. When we were outside the entrance to the cave, I gave the boy the $100 he originally asked for. I explained to him that the scroll was worth more than that, but that's all the money I could afford to give him. He explained that he was simply very grateful that I had given him the full amount to feed his family with.

CHAPTER 2

OVERNIGHT STAY WITH FRIENDS

We walked back to the village to pick up my Jeep, and on the way, I asked the boy if he knew of a good place to stay for the night. Nodding, he said I could stay with him and his family for the night.

"What would your parents think?"

"They would think that you're going to bring them some food to eat."

"Now that," I said, "would be a good trade-off." On the way to the area of the village that housed several squat huts for the residents, we stopped at the marketplace. I bought some bread, some vegetables and some fish. The boy said it would be a feast for them, and his mother was a very good cook.

When we arrived at his home, I parked my Jeep in front of the small mud building. The boy hopped out with a smile. "I will go in and tell my mother and father that you are here." They came to the door and welcomed him in.

It was a small place divided into four cubicles. The living room and kitchen were in the front and two bedrooms in the back. The toilet was also out back. They showed me where I could put my bag and where I could sleep for the night. I learned the boy's name was Gabriel. Gabriel did odd jobs around the village to help buy food. His father was a stonemason by trade, but he had been injured and could not work very much, on the few occasions there was any work at all. The mother was indeed a good cook; I was surprised at her ability to make so few ingredients so delicious. We all talked until it was time for me to retire. I was anxious to look at the scroll but this was not the place or the time. Tomorrow I would be in Cairo. I would be there for several days; and settled for inspecting it then.

My family back in the States was very prosperous in the textile business in the Carolinas. My father was sponsoring this exploration trip. For the last two years I had been researching and reading old manuscripts. I looked over and translated hundreds of wall paintings and carvings, looking for clues to locations where the kings, pharaohs and princes of Egypt were entombed. I had found some very interesting clues and I was using this trip to follow up on them.

The next morning Gabriel's mother fixed breakfast for us. It consisted of some sort of sweet jelly and bread. I took Gabriel with me to the marketplace and purchased some more food for him and his parents. They had been so gracious that it was the least I could do before departing. About 10 o'clock that morning, I was on my way.

CHAPTER 3

CONTINUING ON TO CAIRO

My trip to Cairo was uneventful. I was to meet a Dr. Alan Smite at the Cairo Museum of antiquities the next morning at 10 o'clock. In the meantime, I would check into the hotel where I had already booked a room. The hotel wasn't a large one, but it was quiet and more importantly, it had enclosed parking for my Jeep. My Jeep contained my tents and camping equipment as well as excavation equipment. The hotel had a very small restaurant containing half a dozen tables for its patrons to sit it. The food was very reasonable if you don't mind the wait. I always had my carry bag with me wherever I went because it had my research documents and my computer inside. Also in my carry bag I had a small solar charger, designed so that anytime I was outside the computer could be charging.

I went up to my room, anxious to check out the papyrus scroll. Very carefully, I unrolled the scroll. To my amazement it was very well preserved; it wasn't cracking apart to become unreadable like so many scrolls I have seen in the past. The papyrus had been treated with some type of oil that did not obliterate the hieroglyphics that were placed on it. I began to translate what was on the papyrus. The hieroglyphics seemed to be directions to the tomb of a high priest of Egypt, and contained a warning that whoever should enter the tomb do so at their peril. The priest and all his belongings were considered to be sorcerous and he was put to death by order of one of the Kings of Egypt. His name was not given on the papyrus. The location was somewhat vague, but it might be enough to get me in the ballpark if I decided to go look. I still had to meet Dr. Smite in the morning, after all. I started looking at my notes from my research again and I began to notice some similarities between location I was going to be heading for tomorrow and the directions given on the papyrus scroll. Looking at one of the four maps that I brought with me, I could see that they were within a mile of each other. This was going to be interesting. I not only had one good lead to the possibility of discovering the tomb of the prince, but another good lead possibly to the tomb of a high priest of Egypt.

CHAPTER 4.

THE MEETING AT THE MUSEUM

The museum where I was to meet Dr. Smite was only a quarter-mile from my hotel. I decided to walk, rather than have the hassle of finding a place to park the Jeep. Dr. Smite was right on time for our arrangement, and I met him in the library. Dr. Smite was a well-known archaeologist who had discovered numerous tombs throughout Egypt. I had met him on several occasions during my travels. We greeted each other and shook hands and sat down at one of the tables. After explaining to him what my mission was on this trip, leaving out the part about the scroll, I informed Dr. Smite that I was going to need a small crew to take to the site to do some digging. Weeks before, I had gotten all the paperwork done completed and approved by the Egyptian antiquities bureaucracy at a substantial cost. Dr. Smite said he would be glad to assist me in recruiting the team that I needed. I told him what hotel I was staying in, and he told me that he would give me a call with the name and number of an Egyptian who assembled excavation crews for a living. After some more pleasantries, we shook hands and departed.
I walked around the museum as I had done on several occasions, and was amazed at some of the things that were found just below the surface of the desert floor not far from where I was standing right now. I was even able to recognize a few items; from discoveries I had made myself.

When I was finished I walked back toward my hotel. I picked up some food along the way. When I got back to my room everything was the way I left it. I sat down again at the table to go over the maps once more. All the landmarks were there. The Ancient Egyptians were pretty crafty, and were very good engineers for their time. I had planned to use surveying equipment to help me plot out where I might need to dig.

The phone to my room rang an hour later. It was a man by the name of Adnan. He had been given my number by Dr. Smite, who had indicated that I may need a digging crew. I asked him if he would be available with a crew starting tomorrow for several days, and if he had transportation for them. He said that he did and he could have a crew of five at the hotel in the morning ready to go. I asked him what the total fee would be per day. He told me it would be $500 per day, half paid in advance. I asked him if he would accept a bank draft from a local bank. He agreed, as long as I went with him to the bank to get the money before we departed for the site. I explained to him that I would not be carrying a large amount of money around with me, just in case I got robbed.

"I understand. The bank opens at 9 in the morning. I will meet you and the crew at the hotel and we will go straight to the bank to get your money, then we'll be heading to find the dig site."

CHAPTER 5.

MAKING CAMP

Adnan and the crew were waiting for me outside the hotel at 9AM. Wordlessly, Adnan followed me to the bank to cash in the bank draft. I gave Adnan an advance for three days in an envelope. I showed him on the map exactly where we were going and he knew already how to get there. I had a GPS receiver with extra batteries so I could never really be lost, but decided to follow him. It was going to take a several hours to get there, some of which was on a road and the rest was over the desert. My Jeep was equipped with very wide tires to accommodate the soft surfaces, but it was still four in the afternoon when we arrived at the general area. I took another half-hour comparing the GPS location with the map location. We were off about a mile, so we drove further to get closer to our destination. Adnan had the crew pitch the tents and set up camp.

While they were doing that, I started walking the area. First I wanted to walk the high ground, and noticed several depressions in the area that could possibly mean they were man-made depressions from digging. Marking them on my excavation map, I walked to them to get the exact GPS location of each. Based on my notes I picked the most likely spot to have the crew start digging into in the morning. The area where we were was a combination of sandy desert with cliffs rising from it here and there. I called Adnan over so that I could show him exactly where to start digging in the morning. We took stakes and marked out the area they would dig to, 10 feet down, before moving on. In other words, if digging found nothing within 10 feet deep, we would go to the next spot.

I still had about an hour before sunset, so took the Jeep and drove it to where I figured the location of the high priest's tomb might be based on the information I obtained from the scroll. I could see nothing unusual from where I was sitting on the valley floor, so I drove over close to the cliffs on one side and started to climb. When I reached the top I could look down upon my Jeep and the area surrounding it. I saw nothing on the floor of the valley, but I did see what appeared to be an opening on the cliff on the far side. It was at least a quarter-mile between here and there. I climbed down from the cliff, and using landmarks I walked directly to the other side. From where I was standing at the base of the second cliff I could see no way to climb to the opening I had noticed, invisible from the ground. The sun was beginning to set by this point, so I decided to get back in the Jeep and head back to camp.

When I got back there was food waiting for me. Adnan told me my tent was set up, with the exception of the equipment that was in the back of the Jeep. I apologized for forgetting about it and set about unloading from the Jeep what needed be put into the tent. I set my computer up with the solar charger in a place where the sun could hit it most of the day, and hooked up my satellite phone along with the Internet adapter for my computer. I was able to get face-to-face with my dad on Skype. I gave him an update, omitting the part about the scroll. I turned in about 9 o'clock, knowing at daybreak the work began.

CHAPTER 6

THE DISCOVERY

I watched them dig for about an hour. Then I went back to the Jeep making sure had some rope in there. Shouting to Adnan to watch the crew, I explained I was going up to look at a possible new site to dig, I should return in a couple of hours, and if I wasn't back by then he needed to come and look for me. When I got back to the base of the cliff, I decided to walk up it from the end and then use the rope to come down to the hole that I saw the day before. Using the Jeep as a marker, I would know where to climb down the road. I found a large boulder tie the rope to at the top. I planned to use the rope to let myself down to where the opening of the cave was—the only way to get to this entrance.

I peered into the cave but it was completely dark and I could only see a few feet in. I untied myself from the rope and let it dangle. It was long enough that I could either go up or down when I finished my search. I reached into my pack, pulled out my flashlight and turned it on. Bending over, I entered the cave. Using my flashlight, I looked very carefully around. I could see some very faint hieroglyphics on the wall, but it was difficult to make out what they were saying. I continued back into the cave about 50 feet before I came to a larger chamber. It was obvious that someone had been here before me. The hieroglyphics on this wall were easier to read. Like on the scroll, there was a warning not to enter the burial tomb. It looked to me like someone had already done that. At the back of my mind I wondered what happened to them, if anything. I could see a chiseled out hole in one part of the wall. It was large enough for a man my size to crawl through. Cautiously, I shone my flashlight through the opening, noticing some artifacts remaining. I crawled through to the other side.

There was a stone platform in the center of the room, which itself was about 20 feet across in either direction. On the stone platform was the bottom of a stone sarcophagus. The top had been removed and was lying broken on the floor. I peered inside. Empty. I looked around the room at the other artifacts that were lying broken or tossed around on the floor. I saw nothing of tremendous value. I shone the light on the walls and began reading some of the hieroglyphs painted there. One portion caught my eye more than any other. The reason the high priest was ordered put to death by the King of Egypt at that time was because the King witnessed the high priest disappear right before his eyes. The king declared him a sorcerer, and ordered that when he reappeared, he was to instantly be put to death. When the sorcerer returned he was found out, and instantly put to death. All of his belongings were buried with him and the tomb sanctified. How could someone just disappear?

I read the hieroglyphics all the way around the room. There was a list on one wall of some of the possessions buried with the high priest. At the bottom of the list it said that they were hidden within the burial chamber. Fortunately, I had a keen sense of observation, which I began using as soon as I crawled into the chamber. I noticed that the sarcophagus bottom seemed to be a little thicker than ones I'd seen before. I walked completely around it two times before I saw what I was looking for, a thin groove at the end of the sarcophagus. On the lid there was a small hole about the diameter of a pencil. I took my penknife and opened the blade, pushing it through the groove. Nothing seemed to happen until I lifted up. As I lifted, a small round metal dowel moved up through the hole at the top. I reached over and grabbed it and pulled at the rest of the way out. It was just a solid metal dowel and nothing more. But it was there for a reason, and now I had to figure out why. I tried pushing the sarcophagus from one end toward the other, and it wouldn't budge. I moved to the side, thinking of pushing it off of the pedestal it was sitting on. I pushed hard on the end where I had removed the dowel. When I did the sarcophagus moved slightly. This gave me some encouragement, so I pushed even harder. The harder I pushed, the more it moved. I had moved it several inches, enough to shine the light down into. There *was* something there, but I couldn't make out what it was. I needed to move the sarcophagus more. I looked around the room and saw the pieces from a broken chair. I used the largest piece as a pry bar to move the sarcophagus enough to get a good look at what was under it.

I could see what appeared to be a role of black cloth. What I could see was in excellent condition, considering the age. I reached in and picked it up, laying it on the top of the pedestal. There were other items in the hidden compartment and I pulled them out one at a time. A small wooden box containing a beautiful ring with a blue emerald embedded in the top of it, a dagger with three emeralds similar to the one on the ring. The last thing I found was a leather bag filled with gold coins. I looked at one of the coins; it looked as if it was minted just yesterday, though I knew it was thousands of years old. Without counting them, I calculated there were about 10 gold coins inside. I shone my light all around under the secret compartment but I could see nothing else.

I began taking a closer look at the items I had removed. The black cloth I unfolded very carefully. I couldn't believe how good a shape it was in. When it was completely unfolded, it appeared to be a cape. I carefully refolded it and placed it aside. I then looked at the dagger. The dagger was in a sheath and it was also profoundly well preserved. There was some hieroglyphics etched onto the blade, but they were so small I could not read it without more light and a magnifying glass. I set the dagger down on top of the cape, and turned my attention to the wooden box with a ring inside. I opened the box to take another look at the beautiful ring. I removed the ring from the box, and with my flashlight I inspected it as best I could. I noticed that on one side there was a small lever. I thought maybe it was a latch or something that would allow the ring to open up. When I pushed the lever to the side nothing happened. I pushed it the other way and still nothing happened. As I looked at the ring I could see no reason for the lever. I placed the ring back in the wooden box and placed it also on top of the cape. I walked around to the other side of the sarcophagus and pushed as hard as I could to get it back to the position it was originally in and I replaced the metal dowel. I looked around the room one last time to ensure I had not overlooked anything. Then I folded the dagger and the wooden box in the cape and placed them into my carry bag. The leather bag of gold, I carefully placed in another compartment. I couldn't believe it had been so easy to find the tomb of an Egyptian high priest. I crawled back through the hole that I'd come through and into the outer chamber.

CHAPTER 7

TAKING STOCK OF THE DISCOVERIES

The sunlight was blinding as I reached the outside once more. It took me several minutes to adjust my eyes so I could see my Jeep down below. Instead of climbing down to the car, I decided to climb back up the rope. I didn't want to leave it dangling down to advertise the location of the tomb. Once I was at the top, I untied the rope from the boulder and rolled the rope up like it was before. I walked to the end of the cliffs and then back around to my Jeep. I placed my carry bag right behind the passenger seat, where I always kept it when it was with me. All the way back to the dig site, I kept thinking about the cape. It was extremely hard for me to believe that the cloth was that well preserved through all those years. I had never in my career seen cloth that well preserved in any of the sarcophagi that I had seen in the past. I doubt anyone would believe me if I told them that the cape was as old as the Ancient Egyptian kings.

CHAPTER 8

GRAVE DIGGERS BEAT US TO THE TREASURE

When I arrived at the dig site, the diggers were sitting around a freshly dug hole. In the center of the hole was another that appeared to be stepped, going down. I looked at Adnan.

"What we got so far?"

"We were waiting for you boss, looks like someone got here before us."

Puzzled, I asked him if it was safe to go in.

"Yes, the sand only goes down about 2 feet and the rest is packed dirt."

He handed me his flashlight and I jumped into the hole then went down the steps. There were 21 steps before I came to a chamber. Adnan had followed me down close behind. As I shone light around the chamber I could see what he meant. Broken vases and crockery littered the floor. I carefully walked the perimeter of the walls to look for any hidden chambers, explaining to Adnan what I was looking for so that he could look as well. He pulled out another flashlight so that he could see better. After thoroughly examining the walls I decided that it was a bust.

We went back up the steps and into the bright sunlight again. By then it was about 2 o'clock in the afternoon. I had the crew began to cover the hole. While they were doing that, I grabbed some stakes and had Adnan follow me to the secondary dig site. We placed the stakes around where we wanted the crew to dig. It took the crew only about an hour to fill the hole, but they needed a rest before starting the next dig. I told them to take an hour's break before attempting the new dig.

CHAPTER 9

INVESTIGATING THE ARTIFACTS

I retrieved my carry bag from the Jeep and went to my tent, where I drank a soda and ate some bread and cheese. I pulled the cape out of my carry bag and unfolded it on one knee, extracting the dagger. I took out my magnifying glass to examine the inscription engraved on the blade. It simply had a picture of a ring and a picture of a cloak. I couldn't fathom the meaning, until I opened up the wooden box to examine the ring again. I was still clueless on what the lever was for. It seemed to have three positions, forward, center and back. No matter which way I pushed, nothing happened. Sighing, I grabbed a magnifying glass and looked on the underside of the ring to find an inscription there similar to that on the dagger. There was a picture of a dagger and a picture of what appeared to be a cloak. Since I had found all three things together with the leather bag of gold. I had to assume they were a set. But for what reason? A ring, a cloak and a dagger? I began to speculate. Back in those days, assassins used daggers. And as legends go they were black as well, because they did most of their work at night. Could the high priest have also been an assassin? That was becoming more and more possible. But what had the ring got to do with anything? Without thinking, I tried placing the ring on my right hand index finger, the only one it would fit on. For a second the ring became warm to the touch. At that same moment I saw out of the corner of my eye the emerald in the dagger and emerald in the ring began to glow slightly and then fade away. I took the ring off and put it back on again and when I did the exact same thing happened, the ring became warm and if the same instance the emerald in the dagger and the ring became brighter for a few seconds and then faded away. That was very strange.

I sat there thinking about what had just happened, and what it meant. I moved the lever forward on the ring, deep in thought, and when I did everything began to shimmer around me. Within milliseconds, the tent I was in had disappeared. I was sitting in my folding chair with the cape and dagger sitting on one knee out in the middle of the desert was no one else around. My Jeep was gone. I stood up to look all around me. Seeing nothing but desert and the cliffs nearby, I sat back down in the chair.

My mind was going crazy. What just happened? I reached down to the ground and picked up the cape and dagger that had fallen there when I stood up. I went over everything I was doing just before everything disappeared step-by-step. I had flipped the lever forward on the ring. The lever was now in the forward position. I moved it back to the center. Everything began to shimmer and again within milliseconds I was back in the tent again. Out of curiosity I moved the lever back on the ring. Again, the tent disappeared. This time it was very cold. I could see all around me and it all looked the same as before, other than the climate. I moved the lever back toward the center slowly and I began to notice the temperature change as I did so. As I stopped the lever short of the center, it became hot again. It appeared that I was moving forward in time. Very slowly, I moved the lever closer and closer toward the center. As I did so I noted small changes in the landscape around me. When I was almost to the center I saw the Jeep and the truck pull up. Finally, the lever was at the center point. I watched the crew outside moving around normally. This was amazing, a ring that could take you forward and backward in time. I was very excited. This must be how the high priest became the high priest. He must have truly been a sorcerer. Then I began to wonder about the other two things, the dagger and the cloak. I unfolded the cloak and put it over my shoulders. It had a hood and I put that over my head. Nothing happened, or so I thought until I looked down at the dagger. The emerald on the dagger had gotten brighter for a second. I reached down and picked it up, and when I did, my arm disappeared. I dropped the dagger in surprise and as soon as it was out of my fingers my arm returned to normal. I reached down to pick up the dagger again and as watched as it happened again. I reached over to my bag and pulled out my mirror. No matter how I moved the mirror I was unable to see a reflection of myself. I laid the dagger back down on the table, and no sooner had I than I became fully visible. Unbelievable!

CHAPTER 10

THE TEST

As a child, I read in a fairy story there was a cloak of invisibility. Never in my wildest dreams would I ever have thought that such a thing was real! Yet, here I am wearing one. I was beginning to understand now. I must have all three objects in my possession at the same time for them to work. To test the theory out I picked up the dagger and became invisible again. I walked out of the tent over to where the men were sitting on their break. None of them appeared to take notice. I walked over to where Adnan sat and stood near him. I knew that he would have had to noticed me if he could see me. I walked back to the tent. I took off the cape and folded it, laid the dagger on the cape and I put the ring back in the wooden box, placing it on the cape, which I folded until it was small enough to fit in my carry bag. I looked at the tent to see the crew getting ready to move over to the new dig site—about 150 yards away from the tents.

CHAPTER 11

10 GOLD COINS

I reached into my bag and pulled out the gold coins. I emptied the bag on the table and began to count and examine all 10 of them. There was a likeness of an Egyptian king on each coin. The backside was exactly the same as the front, and lacked dating of any kind. I went to put the coins back into the leather bag, but when I picked it up it seemed to have something in it, I emptied it out on the table to find another 10 gold coins. My excitement grew as I experimented with the leather bag. I put all of the coins back into the bag. And then when I tipped the bag again, only 10 coins came out, but it instantly refilled itself with 10 more coins. I picked up the bag, and sure, enough there were 10 coins in the bag in addition to the 20 on the table. I placed all of the coins back into the bag. This was truly amazing. The owner of this to the bag would always be wealthy. I placed the pouch back into my carry bag. I would have to be very careful not to let any of this stuff get into the wrong hands.

CHAPTER 12

PUTTING THE ARTIFACTS TO THE TEST

Putting my carry bag over my shoulder, I walked out of the tent and up to where the crew was digging. I stood next to Adnan, who asked if the men could stop for the night in another hour. I told him that he was in charge of the crew, and that he could make those decisions. As I watched them dig a thought came to me. At some point in time, Ancient Egyptian slaves had dug every tomb in this area. I walked back to my tent, opened the carry bag and unfolded the cape, removing the ring box. I took the ring out and put it on my finger before carefully folding the cape away. Still inside my tent, I moved the lever on the ring slightly forward. Everything began to shimmer before the tent disappeared. Staying in the exact same position, I looked up the valley to where the men had been digging. Of course they were long gone. I moved the lever forward very slowly and as I watched I could see men digging here and there. These must be the thieves that broke into the tombs. I continued to move the lever forward. As I did so I would stop whenever I saw a burial procession, taking note of where the tomb was located. I counted three, one of which was a very large procession and I paid particular attention to. When I thought I'd seen enough, I began to move lever back to the center position, and back to the present. I placed the ring back in the box and put it back into the fold of the cape and replaced this in my carry bag.

I walked over to the Jeep and picked up the hammer and four wooden stakes. I walked back up to where the workers were digging, and beckoned to Adnan to follow me. I walked up to where I had seen the burial procession enter the tomb. There was no indication at all, but I knew that there was a tomb here. This time, I put the wooden stakes a little further apart, just so I wouldn't miss the entrance. It was at the base of the cliffs on the right-hand side of the valley. Adnan looked skeptical, but said nothing. I told him to go back down and tell the crew to stop digging for the day. In the morning we would dig here instead.

CHAPTER 13

NEW DISCOVERY

The next morning the crew began digging in the new location. About two hours into the digging there were indications that there was something here. As they dug I became more and more excited. I knew that tomb robbers had not desecrated this tomb. Finally they came to a solid stone block, which covered the entrance to the tomb. The diggers placed ropes around the block, and with the help of the truck were able to pull it one side of it away from the entrance. It appeared the rock slab was on hinges. The diggers cleaned until three or four men could move it freely. Adnan handed me a flashlight and I went into the entrance. After about 10 feet there was a small cavern and at each end there was a tunnel, large enough for two men standing side-by-side to walk through. We went to the right side first and followed it around about 20 yards until it came to a larger chamber. This chamber was filled with artifacts belonging to the Egyptian king. In the middle of the far wall was another opening. We walked over and went in. There in the center was the stone sarcophagus that held the mummified remains of the king. Everything that we saw was exactly as it was placed in the tomb when he died. We left the room and returned to the surface.

I allowed Adnan to take the crew down into the tomb to see what we had discovered, reminding them not to touch anything. I asked Adnan to have the crew pitch a tent around the entrance and place a guard to make sure no one went into the tomb. In order to document the find I had to send for the Egyptian official who had to be present before anything could be removed. I sent Adnan back to Cairo in the truck to notify the official, and also had him pick up a load of wood and packing materials and bring them back to the camp.

CHAPTER 14

THE OFFICIAL'S ARRIVAL

The Egyptian antiquities official wasted no time in getting to the site. The next morning at 10 o'clock he had arrived with an assistant. I sent Adnan back in the Cairo to get more wood and packing material, and had him rent a trailer large enough to haul as much as possible of the items we were packing up. The Egyptian official was very pleasant. I had met him before, and he knew that I wasn't just out for making money. After all, the way this worked was pretty simple. Everything that came out of the tomb belonged to the Egyptian government, but because we found it we had the right to exhibit it, and this would form our profit. Of course, there was also the notoriety of having discovered it.

Over the course of the next four days, everything in the tomb was photographed in its original position before it was removed and carefully packed and catalogued. Then it was placed in the trailer or on the truck to be taken to the museum warehouse where it would be re-catalogued. Photos were taken of every wall inside the tomb. The Egyptian official had assigned armed guards for both the tomb and the convoys taking the discovery back to Cairo. When all was said and done, I paid Adnan and his crew the balance I owed them and topped it off with a very generous bonus. I told him that it was possible I could use them again in the near future.

CHAPTER 15

HEADING FOR THE STATES

Now that the tomb was in the hands of the Egyptian government and all the procedure was completed. I began to plan how I was to get out of the country with the items I had taken from the tomb of the high priest. I returned the Jeep to the rental company, paid the hotel bill and booked my flight back to the States.

The plane left at 3pm, later in the day. I arrived at the airport an hour early and checked in all my luggage except my carry bag. I went into the men's bathroom, entered a stall and took out the cape, dagger and ring. I put the ring on just in case I needed it, sheathed the dagger in my belt, slipped the cape over my shoulders and put the hood over my head. Immediately, I became invisible. I opened the stall, and as I did, I look at the mirrors. I could see the stall door opening and nothing else. I knew I was truly invisible. I left the bathroom and went toward the screening area. I walked past the metal detectors and luggage checkers, went up to the boarding area and found the lockers. I went into the bathroom removed everything and placed it all into my carry bag. Then I went back to the lockers and placed the carry bag in one memorizing the number and removed the key once I had checked it was locked. I then walked back toward the security waiting area. I knew that the people leaving the boarding area could not be screening staff. I put the key on my key ring, and waited for my flight to be called. When it was, I got in line with everyone else to be screened before heading to the boarding area.

Once I was through the screening area, I removed the key from my keychain, opened the locker and pulled out my carry bag. I then waited to be boarded on the plane. The flight was a long one, and I slept through much of it. When I arrived in New York City, I repeated the process in order to get through customs, and then was able to safely book a flight to my home in Washington DC.

CHAPTER 16

UPS AT THE RESCUE

The flight to New York arrived at my destination in four hours, after which I hailed a cab to the nearest UPS store. I had a driver wait for me while I went in to the store. I purchased a box and packing material big enough to accommodate the leather bag of coins and the cloak, as well as the dagger and the box with the ring in it. I carefully packed everything in the box. I then taped the box up, wrapping it in heavy duty wrapping paper, and taped this up again. I put a label on the box addressing it to my apartment to be delivered by the next morning before 10 o'clock. I put the receipt in my wallet and went back out and got into the cab. The cabbie took me back to the airport and I paid him twice what the meter showed. He handed me a card with his number and name, telling me if I ever needed a cab to anywhere when I was in New York City to call him. I retrieved my bags and checked them in for my new flight the Washington DC. The flight was leaving in less than an hour so I decided to go to the boarding area and wait there. They had a sandwich shop, a coffee shop and a gift shop. I ordered a grilled ham and cheese sandwich and a soda. By the time I finished, the loudspeaker announced the boarding of my flight. I boarded the plane and got a seat by the window. The flight wasn't a long one. It seemed like by the time we got to cruising altitude; we were heading back down again for the landing. When the plane landed I rounded up my entire luggage and hailed a cab to take me home. I asked the cabbie to give me a hand carrying the luggage into my house for a reward. When we had finished, I paid the cabbie the regular fare and tipped him $40.

CHAPTER 17

ANXIETY

Anxiety was getting to me while I was waiting for UPS to arrive 10 o'clock. I had already taken a shower, eaten breakfast and unpacked most of my luggage while I was waiting. The clock showed 9:50 AM. When I looked again it was 9:52 AM. Time seemed to be dragging; my anticipation of getting the artifacts back into my hands was overwhelming. At 9:58 AM the UPS van pulled up in the driveway. It was like a great weight had been taken off my shoulders when the UPS driver handed me the package. I signed for it and took it back into the house to open it.

Once I had the box opened and had pulled out the contents, I began to check them over again. The ring I was especially interested in. Looking at the ring carefully with a more powerful magnifying glass was interesting. Other than the lever and the inscription on the inside, there was nothing significant about the ring, which would not function without having it on your finger and the other two items in your possession. I noticed the lever had a small groove on the top. I pushed on the lever, but it did not move. I grabbed it with two fingers and dragged it, and the lever pulled out one notch to display another groove. I pushed it back in so it displayed only the one. Evidently, the ring had other functions besides time travelling. I decided to see what it did, so I put on the cloak and stuck the dagger into my belt, pushing the ring on my index finger. My mind raced with thoughts of the high priest and what he did with these items. When I pulled out the lever, everything once again began to shimmer as my surroundings changed.

I was in a temple of some sort. A priest knelt in front of an altar, performing some sort of ceremony. In his hand was a dagger exactly like the one that I now had in my belt. The priest was preparing to impale the dagger into the victim tied to the altar. I stood there and watched for a few seconds once the priest impaled the sacrifice. It became a bloody affair and I decided not to watch any longer. I thought about how to get back to my house, I flicked the lever back in and instantly I was back in my kitchen table.

I was stunned at the implications of what I had seen. I just witnessed the high priest murder a victim on an altar. The high priest must have been a very wicked sorcerer indeed. There was another pressing question in my mind. How I had managed to go there of all places? Then I remembered that I was thinking of the high priest when I pulled out the lever. I decided to try another experiment. I thought to myself about my front yard and how the grass had grown. I pulled the lever. In seconds, was on my front lawn standing in the grass. Now I understood how the ring worked. It appeared that I could go anywhere that I was thinking of when the lever was moved. To prove the point, I thought of my backyard, moved the lever and I was there. I then thought of the Washington Monument and did the same. Instantly I was standing inside it. Finally, I thought of my kitchen at my home and pushed the lever and found myself standing next to the kitchen table once more. This was amazing. I knew right then that my life was about to change.

I removed the cloak and folded it again. In my closet I had a beautiful leather briefcase that my father had given me last year. It was just the right size to accommodate the artifacts.

CHAPTER 18

MY SPECIAL HOUSE

When I bought this house—fully furnished—at auction following its foreclosure, I found that not only had the previous owner died without an heir, but also that he was an interesting combination of eccentric and paranoid. He had built into this house a safe room, but died and left no indication about how to get into it. The realtor knew that it was a safe room from the deeds, but could not show it to me. It took me a week of searching to figure out how to get in. It was all in a book on the shelf. I had removed every book on the bookshelf except one and it seemed to be stuck. As I pulled it, the bookshelf began to move, revealing a door that opened by sliding it to one side. The safe room also had a trap door in the floor and ceiling to allow access to the upper floor and the basement. He had put a lot of thought into it. The basement section of the safe room opened up into another hidden room where a large safe was contained.

The wall in the basement was lined with cinderblocks that were on a sliding track and could only be pushed open from the inside. From the outside, there was no indication of an opening in the wall. Upstairs, too, had a secret door behind a bookshelf. The house on the whole had been perfect for me even before these discoveries, and though it needed some repairs on the outside, it was otherwise in excellent condition.

CHAPTER 19

I'M RICH

The safe in the basement was locked when I first found it. I played with a combination for a short time, but quickly started looking around for any clue that might lead to the combination. While I was searching, a small spider dangled near my face. When I swatted it away I happened to look up. There was a small sliver of paper wedged into a crack where the wood came together in the rafters above. I pulled the piece of paper out of its hiding place and open it up. It was the combination! 32 to the left, 6 to the right, 21 to the left, zero to the right. I pulled the handle and the safe opened right up. To my amazement, there were stacks and stacks of money of all denominations. There were about 20 gold bars, one bag of gold coins and a stack of bearer bonds. There was also a deed to some 100 acres of land in Maryland on the outskirts of Washington DC.

I called my realtor and had her check to see if the land had been sold for taxes or not. She told me the auction for the land would be the following Friday on the court house steps. I had my bank draw up a letter that would allow her to bid on the property as high as she needed to go in order to win. As luck would have it, it was snowing on the day of the auction and I guess all the potential bidders stayed home. The taxes owed on the land were only $15,000, and since no one else was bidding she bought the property for me for that amount plus some fees. Property anywhere in that part of Maryland would normally go for $10-$20,000 an acre any day of the week, so I was more than pleased with the purchase. Since the previous owner had no heirs, I was not inclined to hand over the money that was in the safe to the state. The bearer bonds alone were worth several million dollars. They were for several multimillion-dollar companies. From looking at all the books and ledgers that he kept, I had to conclude that the man had been a stockbroker, or working in a brokerage company in some manner. He clearly didn't like banks.

Snapping out of my reverie, I decided I wanted to find out more about the coins from the pouch. I removed two, and then I emptied the pouch out on the kitchen table to see if it still contained 10 coins, which it did. I put 10 coins back into the pouch, and placed the two remaining coins in my pocket. I opened the safe room and put the briefcase in it.

CHAPTER 20

HISTORY LESSON ABOUT THE GOLD COINS

After hiding the artifacts, I headed to the garage to make sure my car would still start. Fortunately it started right up, and I decided to let the car run for a few minutes him. I would head over to a precious coin dealer that I knew to get an idea of the timeframe of the coins, supplementing my research about the era that the high priest lived in. I knew it had to be very early in Egyptian history because the hieroglyphics I saw in the tomb mentioned a King and not a Pharaoh. Maybe the coin dealer could give me a better idea.

I locked up the house, set the alarm, and headed over to see the coin dealer. At the coin dealer's shop, he greeted me and asked me how my expedition had gone. I told him the short version of the story, leaving out the part about the high priest. I reached into my pocket and pulled out the two gold coins and handed them to him. His eyes lit up as if it was Christmas.

"I was wondering," I said, "Could you date these coins for me?"

The coin dealer looked at me. "Are these coins for sale?"

I told him I didn't know if I was going to sell them or not. "It depends on the importance. I need to find out more about them."

"I can give you a little history on these coins. They are very—and I mean *very*—rare. I've only seen one personally. But the rare coin catalog indicates only a handful are known to exist. And they are coveted by wealthy coin collectors who buy them just because they can. This is a Gold Daric of Pharaoh/king Nectanebo II, from the time period 342 to 361BC. This is not just a common coin. It was only used by the upper class. The commoners were forbidden to have them, as the legend goes. Legend also says that that most of the coins were lost at sea in a great storm somewhere along Egyptian coast. That's about as close to the full history as you're going to get."

"How much would they be worth?" I asked the coin dealer.

"They would be almost priceless. I would say several million dollars each, should you auction them off. Of course, you would have to prove their authenticity."

"And how would I do that?" I asked.

"Not very easily. You would have to have several experts test the coins to verify their authenticity to the era from which they came. And you would have to prove that they did not come from Egypt. The Egyptians claim all artifacts coming from their country, no matter when or where, belong to them, and they will make every effort to have them returned. However, if they were found somewhere outside of Egypt and you can prove it, then they have no claim."

"How much would they be if they were melted down?"

The coin dealer looked back at me in shock. "You're not going to melt them down are you?"

"Oh no," I said, "What I meant to say was, if they were melted down what would they be worth?"

"If they were melted down by a refinery and put in ingot form they would be worth whatever the going rate is for the spot price of gold; somewhere between $1200 and $1300 an ounce."

 I asked the coin dealer if he thought he could find a buyer for the coins without having to go through all the trouble of authentication. The coin dealer told me it might be possible, but he would have to 'put out some feelers' to see who might be interested. I gave the two coins to him for safekeeping, telling him that if he could find a buyer there would be a substantial commission, as long as he handled the complete transaction and left my name out. He understood my meaning.

CHAPTER 21

A GOOD DEED

I drove home wondering what my next move might be. Although I had taken the artifacts from Egypt, I really didn't consider myself a thief. I would rather that I have control over them than turn them over to some government bureaucrat in Egypt, though. They could easily fall into the wrong hands and God only knew what would happen then. I was not an assassin, either, although that was what they appeared to be used for. I would just have to keep thinking of a proper use for the artifacts. I thought about things like going back in time to watch the birth of Jesus, or putting myself into the book depository in Dallas Texas to prevent the assassination of JFK. I didn't know what the implications were if I changed anything when I went back in time. I would have to figure that out as I went along. I wondered if there was anyone else in the world that was able to do the things that I could do now.

Now that I was independently wealthy, I was free to go in any direction that I pleased. While I was pondering about what I was going to do with myself next, a thought crossed my mind. If I carried a camera with me while I was wearing the cloak, would I still be able to record anything that I saw with it? When I got home, I retrieved the artifacts from the briefcase and put the cape and ring on, then I put the dagger in my belt, triggering my invisibility. I picked up my smartphone, which instantly became invisible also. From memory I pushed the camera button to take a photo than I laid the phone down to see if it took or not. To my surprise, it had! I laid the dagger down on the table, making myself visible again and set the phone to record, making sure I knew where to hit to start and stop recording. I picked up the dagger and disappeared from view before pressing record. I recorded for several minutes, walking around the house, then went back into the kitchen and set the dagger down on the table so I could see the phone. I rewound the recording and hit the play button. Everything I recorded was there. I now knew what I was going to do for my next project.

I had a good camera, but I wanted something smaller and more compact, with simple controls. The local camera shop should stock just the right camera for my needs. I found one that was as near perfect for my next project as one could get. A high definition camera designed for sports recording, it was small and could be worn on a strap wherever you wanted to mount it. You could use either the controls on the camera or the convenient remote control buttons on a small controller. It had several buttons, but the only three I would need were the power, start recording, and stop recording buttons. I purchased the camera and twenty 8-gigabyte SD cards to fit the camera. When I got home I tried it out and it worked like a champ.

I was now an unofficial investigative reporter. In theory, I could crack any case wide open by filming what ever happened as it was being committed to prove innocence or guilt. So that's what I set out to do. I watched the news, and read the papers and searched the Internet to find a simple yet worthy project to start with. In the local paper I found a story of a local janitor who was being held without bond for the brutal murder of a female tenant in the building where he worked. The story gave the address and apartment number where the woman was murdered, as well as the time and date that it had occurred, two days before. Printed to the left of the story was a photo of the room where she was murdered. First, I would need to go and see the place where she was murdered, so I could shift there if I needed to. This should be a simple operation. I grabbed my briefcase with the artifacts and my new camera and drove to the location mentioned in the newspaper story.

It was a six-storey apartment building. The murder victim had lived on the second floor, apartment 201. I walked up the stairs to the second floor and found the apartment. It still had yellow police tape across the door with a sign that said 'Crime Scene: Authorized Personnel Only.' I reached over and turned the doorknob and the door opened. So much for security. I ducked under the tape and entered the room, closing the door behind me. I went into the bedroom where the murder occurred and removed the ring from the briefcase, placing it on my finger. I put the camera on my head, then the cape on and the dagger in my belt, becoming invisible. I stood next to the window where I would be out of the way and could get a good view of everything that occurred. I then moved the lever on the ring very slowly backward. Everything moved as if on rewind. When I got to the part just before the woman was attacked, I stopped and started recording the event.

I watched as she got undressed for bed and into her nightgown. She had been asleep for several minutes when her bedroom door, which was already open, begin to open wider, I could see a white male with a black mustache and goatee enter the room. He leaned over the bed and placed a gloved hand over the woman's mouth. She began to struggle.

"If you scream I'm going to kill you, do you understand me?" The man hissed, tightening his grip.

Frightened, she nodded yes. He told her he was only there for sex and if she gave him no trouble he would leave her alive. She complied, weeping, and he pulled up her nightgown and pulled down his pants and began to rape her roughly. She began to whimper and he told her to shut up. When she failed to stop, he grabbed her by the throat with his gloved hands and began to strangle her. She put up as good as fight as she could but it was not enough. The killer put his pants back on and looked around the room. He found her purse and took out her wallet, stuffing it into his jacket pocket. The woman gave out a soft moan and the rapist picked up the lamp on the nightstand, hitting her head and face several times until he knew she was dead.

I followed him downstairs to the first floor when he left her apartment. He looked into the wallet, removed some money, and then threw the wallet down the stairs to the basement. He then started walking toward the parking lot around the corner. I followed him to his car, still filming. I captured his tag number in the video as he drove off, and then walked behind the building where I could not be seen and began removing the cape and dagger. I placed them in the briefcase—which I had held under my arm—then reached over and moved the ring lever back to the center, bringing me back to the present. I walked back to my car so I could go home and review the video. It made me sick to watch it, but I steeled myself to gain justice for the victim and the wrongly accused man. I made a copy of the video on two CDs, addressing one to the newspaper that carried the story and one to the Homicide Department of the Washington DC Police Department. Once the story ran about the wrongful incarceration of the janitor, the police department acted swiftly and tracked down and arrested the real killer. The janitor was released and publically exonerated. No one seemed to question the validity of the video or where it had come from.

I felt good about what I had done, although guilty for not saving the woman. I don't know what would have happened if I had decided to step in and stop the killer. I reasoned that it had already happened, so it was something that I should not try to prevent. However, if I could keep something from happening in the future, it probably would not change anything that had already occurred. I needed to find something different to focus on, something that had broader implications.

CHAPTER 22

INVESTIGATING THE HIGH PRIEST

I started thinking about the high priest, and how he became high priest. I wanted to find out if he really was an assassin or not. The more thought I gave to it, the more I was determined to find out. I had no idea where he was from, or who the King was that had him killed. I only had one clue.

 I pulled on the cape and tied the dagger to my belt, slotting the ring on my right index finger. I thought of the dig site in the desert and pulled the lever everything began to shimmer. Within a millisecond, I was standing in the desert. I began to pull the lever back, taking me back in time. When I got close to the period where the burial processions moved towards the different tombs, I slowed down to a crawl. When the burial procession came with the high priest I slowed down even further.

I now saw how they managed to get to the tomb. They put blocks on the ground and stacked them in such a way that they were able to walk right up to the entrance. When they finished burying the high priest, the work crews dug out a trench and laid all of the blocks back into it, before covering everything. You would never have known that the blocks were even buried there. I assumed that they might use the casket they took away to bury someone else. When they were all finished, I followed them back. It was a long walk, at least 5 miles before we arrived at a city of beautiful buildings and organized thoroughfares. The procession broke apart at the gate, where the workers separated from the higher-class personnel. I picked up the one I thought was in charge of everything and followed him and his numerous assistants. They went to what appeared to be a palace with beautiful statues and plants all around. The floor was tiled in vibrant colors and intricate designs. I followed them to the throne room, where they bowed in front of the King or Pharaoh. I wasn't sure which it was at this point. The leader rose from his knees and gave his report. He called the person sitting on the throne a king. He reported to the King that the high priest and all his belongings had been buried secretly in the desert, and that his name was not mentioned anywhere. He then handed a scroll to the King's assistant, which was opened and read to the king. It was the same scroll that I owned. When he finished reading it to the king, he was instructed to take the scroll and hide it from all eyes.

CHAPTER 23

THE CUNNING KING

I decided to stand next to the throne and go back further in time to see if the high priest would show up. Very slowly, I moved the lever on the ring, watching everything as I did so. Within a few seconds, I saw a procession of priests come before the throne. The high priest was leading the procession. To either side of me there were archers who were aiming their bows and arrows toward the high priest. The King was calling the high priest a sorcerer and an assassin because he suspected the high priest and something to do with the murder of his oldest son. The priest was denied it, but the King raised his hand and a prisoner was brought in and put at the foot of the throne. The prisoner was one of the high priest's followers. The King had had him tortured until he told them what he knew about the assassination of the Kings son. The prisoner had said that the high priest was the assassin and that he could come and go unseen to the naked eye.

The high priest, knowing that he could not talk his way out of situation, simply vanished right in front of the King. That verified that the prisoner was telling the truth, and he was released. The King also ordered that should the high priest be seen again, he was to be immediately put to death without hesitation. The King then posted several more archers around the throne. The king seemed to be a very wise man, or had experienced this before. He ordered a powder placed all around the throne and at every entrance. Should someone enter the throne room, they would leave footprints on the floor. Sure enough, the high priest returned, leaving his footprints. The archers didn't hesitate. He was shot several times, and as he fell to the ground he dropped the dagger, making him visible again. The King had him removed, ordering that he be buried in the tomb and all of his possessions hidden so that they would not be found. I decided that I'd seen enough.

I went forward in time just enough that all the powder was gone from the floor along with the archers, just in case I could get shot myself. I walked outside and went back in time enough to follow the high priest's followers to their place of worship. Groups were talking among themselves about what happened at the throne. They walked to a stone building with elaborate designs all around the door. I followed them in. In the back was the altar that I'd seen the high priest perform a sacrifice on. There was no one tied there now. I decided to stand near the altar and go back in time far enough for the priest to appear. I resolved to follow the priest to see if he really did assassinate the King's son. Before long, the high priest appeared. He spoke in front of his followers and then departed out a side entrance.

CHAPTER 24

THE HIGH PRIEST'S CHAMBER

I followed him to the entrance into a smaller building and watched as he pulled a secret lever that opened a hidden panel in the wall. A portion of the wall moved aside and he and I walked through the gap. He pulled the lever on the other side, and the opening closed up. He walked down a passage and entered a door to a larger chamber. This chamber contained all sorts of glass beakers and jars. To one side, there was a wall with chains attached to it, occupied by two men. There were a large number of scrolls that appeared to be ordered on a shelf against one wall.

I watched the high priest as he worked at the table. He was working on some kind of powder. He put the powder in a small blowgun to about 10 inches long, and blew the powder into the face of one of the prisoners, who immediately went limp. His chest continued to rise and fall steadily, and he seemed to be asleep. The high priest went back to the table and picked up another blowgun. He blew this powder into the face of the second man. The second man's eyes had been darting back and forth, but after the powder was blown into his face his eyes glazed over and he stared straight ahead. The high priest commanded the man to stand up. When he stood up the high priest commanded the man to hold out his hand. Obediently, the prisoner held out his hand. The high priest took out his dagger and sliced the man's hand, but there was no indication he was in pain. The high priest placed a clay bowl under the man's hand so the blood would drip into it. From my left I heard a female voice.

"Okto, I just received word that the king's son has been assassinated."

"Yes, my queen, I know. Our plan is working! If the king has no heir to the throne then you will become the ruler, and we will be free to be together."

The queen walked over to the high priest and gave him a passionate hug and kiss. "Okto" she said, "When the king is no more, we shall rule more than this kingdom, we shall rule all of the southern lands, all the way to the sea. No other king will be able to stand before us and hinder the way."

"You are most devious, my dear!"

"And you are most cunning" said the queen.

"Look," said Okto. "My new potions are working. This one was hastened to slumber with just a breath. And the other one will be an obedient slave to do my bidding, if he lives from the cut on his hand. I doubt he will live, with so much of his lifeblood draining from his body. "

I walked over to the table where he was preparing the potions. He had a vial of each. One was greenish, and the other was almost black. I did not know which one, had which effect. I would have to go back a little to find out. They would be very useful later regardless. I left them where they were for now. There were several other potions on the table as well, and it would be nice to know what they were for. I stood out of the way again and went back further to see if I could find out what they were used for.

Evidently, the queen spent a lot of time in the high priest's chamber. I started recording with the camera as he picked each of the vials up to show the queen.

"This one will cause death within a few heartbeats. This one will paralyze the strongest man with just one intake of breath. Here is one of my favorites. It will make any man forget even his name."

"Okto, how are you able to make such wondrous potions?"

"On my travels, I discovered a book with many of them in it and I have been able to discover others on my own."

He went to a shelf behind the worktable and moved a shelf divider to the side, revealing a secret compartment in the wall. The queen was reaching in to get the book, but Okto grabbed her arm before she could. "My dear queen, I would not want to lose you so soon. Watch." He picked up a large spoon used for stirring concoctions and tossed it into the opening. The spoon was cut in half before it was all the way in. "I'm sure you would not fare well with just one hand." He turned the shelf divider to on its side to disarm the trap, and reached in. It was a very thick book, almost 4 inches. "I discovered this book in the tomb of a very powerful high priest. It took some time to translate some of the ancient language to the present. In the process I learned three languages, and parts of several more."
"You are very creative," the queen whispered.
"And you," Okto said confidently "are very lucky." He placed the book back into the opening and closed and reset the trap.

CHAPTER 25

WINDFALL DISCOVERY

I got what I needed and made another discovery at the same time, the book. I watched them for a short time longer until they went over to a long couch and made love. To give them privacy, I moved the lever on the ring forward a little to a time when no one was in the chamber. I picked up a woven bag and placed the potions I had heard Okto explain into the bag, I made sure they would not spill their contents, then went to the shelf on the wall and pushed aside the divider, throwing a stir stick in first to test it. When nothing happened, I reached in and retrieved the book. There were also other things there, all of which I took. I reset the trap and made everything as it was before as best as I could before leaving the chamber. I wanted to be outside of the building before I came forward in time to the present. I had my small GPS unit and wanted to see exactly where this city was located. When I got outside I checked the GPS, but it wasn't working. How stupid of me to think it would work so far back in the past! I moved the lever to the center position on the ring. In seconds I was back in my original time period. I looked around and could see no trace that a thriving city had ever been here. I checked the GPS and recorded the location in order to dig up some more information on the city later. I began thinking of my kitchen at home and pushed the lever on the ring. When the shimmering stopped I was standing in front of my kitchen table. I was very tired, and had to drag myself put everything in the safe room and secure it. I then went to my bedroom and was asleep in seconds.

CHAPTER 26

A DEAL WITH THE COIN DEALER

The phone woke me up. It was already 10:15 AM in the morning. It was the coin dealer with a potential buyer, if I truly wanted to sell the coins. I asked him how much he was offered.

"Only six million for one of the coins."

I asked him how much he thought the coin should bring. "Not less than ten million, based on the rarity."

"Okay. I'll make you a deal you cannot refuse. You get me eight million for one of the coins, and I will give you the other coin as your commission."

I could hear the coin dealer fumbling with the phone. He had apparently dropped it. "Did I hear you correctly? You said if I get you eight million for the coin, you would give me, without any strings attached the other coin for my commission?"

"Yes, that's what I said. There is one string attached. You must not tell anyone where you got the coins. If you can live with that then we can do business."

"I'm sure we can work it out," he said, "I will call you when and if we have a deal with a buyer." I thanked him before hanging up.

CHAPTER 27

FABULOUS TREASURE

I got up the next morning, eager to look through the finds of the day before. I dressed and went down to the kitchen for some coffee and toast. While the coffee was brewing, I went to the safe room and retrieved the woven bag and my camera. I removed each item and set it on the table beside the bag. The book was first. There was then a leather bound pouch with paper in it. I stopped. Paper! I opened the pouch to reveal documents that were in hand written in Italian by Leonardo da Vinci and they were dated 1489 AD. As best as I could tell, they were lab notes and writings with drawings. I put them back in the leather pouch and set it on top of the book. There were also two scrolls. They were like new. I could read some of what was written on them. One was about a crucifixion of a king of the Jews and the other was of his rising from the dead. This was mind bending; here was a detailed description of the crucifixion of Jesus Christ and detailed rundown of what happened after he had risen from the dead. These would be the most valuable two items in the world today.

I wondered why the high priest wanted them and then it dawned on me that he was interested in *how* Jesus was raised from the dead. I'm sure that information would be very important for someone like Okto the high priest. I had to go back and find out where Okto got the ring, cape, and dagger. I began to wonder about how I could get to them before he did and what the implications would be. I remember him mentioning getting the book from a great high priest of ancient times, He would have to gotten them from his own time, because before he got them he could not move in time. And it had to be within travelling distance from his home city. That narrowed it down considerably.

I picked the book up to see if it gave any clues as to its origin or of the great high priest. Onias was the only name that came up. I went to my computer and searched for that name. It was of a high priest from Jerusalem. Okto would have access to the burial location as a high priest, and if not, he would have certainly gotten it by persuasion. I could find no indication of where he was buried, but I guessed it had to be somewhere near Jerusalem. Then I thought about the other items I brought back from Okto's chamber. I went back over to the table where I placed the items.

CHAPTER 28

THE DIRECTIONS

There were several flat papyrus sheets. I looked at each of them and there it was! On the last one I picked up was the original copy the scribe had written to document the location of their high priest. His body was removed from Jerusalem and brought to the Valley of the Kings, near to where my dig had been. From the description given I would be able to go back and follow the burial procession right to the tomb. I placed everything back in the safe room and took only my carry bag with flashlight, GPS receiver and a small crowbar, just in case I might have needed it. Not forgetting the camera, I put the ring on and the dagger in my belt and draped the cape over my shoulders and head. I again thought about the place of my dig and pulled the lever on the ring.

When the shimmering stopped, I was there under the hot sun. I looked all around and could only see the gate and sign the government put up around the tomb I had recently discovered. I moved the lever back again until I began to see activity. First it was the grave robbers, then the processions of the king's burial parties. I knew that the tomb would be on the left side of the valley because there was an entry on the papyrus that mentioned the sun rising over a cleft and moving down to where the tomb was located. The valley was from north to south, so that made the sun rise from the right. The shadow must therefore drop on the left side where the tomb should be. I directed my attention to the processions that had burials on that side of the valley.

There were two that met the prerequisites that I had set. It wouldn't be a large procession and it wouldn't be very fancy. I followed the smaller of the two, being careful not to get too close to the procession because someone might notice my footprints in the sand. I noticed that some of the party was barefoot, so I sat down and pulled off my shoes, burying them in the sand where I could find them later. They set up a tent and the diggers began to dig the tomb. I moved forward slightly to when the tomb was finished and followed them in for the final burial. They had done a good job. I stood as far out of the way as I could and watched everything they did. I saw them lift the sarcophagus onto a small platform. They removed the top from it and started placing items around the edges of the mummified body of the high priest. All the items were wrapped, but I could tell by the shape of some of them that one was probably a dagger.

CHAPTER 29

BURIED ALIVE

When they were finished, they had some sort of ceremony and one by one departed. I heard the diggers begin to put blocks of stone at the entrance to block entry. Soon, it was completely dark inside the tomb. Silently being buried alive was the hardest thing I have ever done. Several minutes after it was pitch black, I turned my flashlight on. I walked over to the sarcophagus and pried off the lid, I pushed it aside and peered in at the items placed around the mummy. I removed them one at a time. The one that looked like a dagger, I removed first. Sure enough, it was the same dagger I had in my belt. I had thought about the problem I might have it I was in possession of both sets of the artifacts, so removed the cloak and set it on the end of the sarcophagus, untied the dagger and placed it on top of the cloak, then I removed the ring and put it there also. I picked up the dagger I had just unwrapped and put it in my belt. I looked for a smaller item and unwrapped it. There was the wooden box with the ring inside. I put the ring on my right index finger and continued looking for the cloak. I chose the item that was about the right size and unwrapped it. I was relieved to see the black cloth of the cloak. I put it on and instantly became invisible. There were other items in the sarcophagus, but rather than take the time to unwrap them, I put them all in my carry bag. I was trying to decide what to do with the artifacts I brought with me. I knew that some time in the future Okto would find this tomb and take them, and I did not want to touch them again. I decided to move forward in time to when Okto dug his way into the tomb to get the artifacts.

Just as I was about to move the lever on the ring, I could hear scraping coming from the entrance to the tomb. Surly they would not be digging this soon? I made sure I was invisible, turned my flashlight off and waited. In about an hour light began to come through the entrance.

CHAPTER 30

OKTO THE HIGH PRIEST, GRAVE ROBBER

After another few minutes, a figure holding a torch moved into the chamber. It was none other than Okto the high priest. He looked around and saw all the wrappings strewn around the sarcophagus and the artifacts on the end of it. He walked around the whole thing two or three times. Then he picked up the dagger and ring, inspecting them both. He put the ring on his index finger then pulled the dagger from its sheath and examined it. Putting it back in the sheath, he attached it to his belt at his waist. Next, he picked up the cloak. He put it over his shoulders and head. He did not become invisible. That was a big relief for me. I watched with baited breath as he discovered the lever on the ring and moved it back and forth, but I was relieved that nothing at all happened. He pulled out the dagger again and examined it again. With a disgusted look on his face he departed. I followed not too far behind. When I got to the entrance, I was appalled at what I saw.

CHAPTER 31

CONFRONTATION, LIFE OR DEATH DECISION

The high priest and four other riders were leaving heading south toward the city I had registered with my GPS. All around me lay the dead bodies of the diggers and priest from the burial procession. Their tent was still up, with the flaps waving in the wind. I walked over to where I had buried my shoes and hurriedly dug them up. I had just put them on when out of the corner of my eye I saw the riders racing back towards me. I was on the high ground and they would have to slow down a lot before they could get to me. I stuck the dagger into the ground at my feet. As soon as I let it go, I became visible again. Okto spotted me immediately and pointed in my direction. They all headed toward me. I held up my hand for them to stop. "

Stop or you shall all die a terrible death!" They all stopped, including Okto. I said "Okto! Yes, Okto, I know your name. You have come here to desecrate my grave. You killed my people, yet I let you live to give you this message. I know of your plan to assassinate the King's son, and to later murder the king himself in order to bring the queen into power. But I tell you this; it will not come to pass. I have warned the king of your wickedness and he will be wary. If you value your lives go now and don't look back!"

The four riders began backing away. Okto did not. We were about twenty yards apart, and he began to take steps toward me. As he did, he pulled out the dagger, and threw the sheath onto the ground. "I am going to kill you instead! You cannot escape me, because like any man you leave footprints in the sand."

"Okto, you are not wise in everything. If you want to live another day you will leave now. If not you will lie on my footprints and they will be the last thing you will see of this world!"

Okto began to rush in my direction; I bent down and picked up the dagger instantly becoming invisible again. He stopped in his tracks about five feet in front of me, looking at the ground. I moved the lever on the ring in while I was thinking of being about ten feet behind him. Before he could blink an eye, I was behind him. "You see, Okto? You do not know everything."

He whirled around to look in my direction, but he could not see me. He again looked at the ground. It registered he was puzzled at the kind of footprints I was leaving—my boots had designs on the soles. "Who are you?" he said.

"I am the one you came here to rob, I am Onias. I died, but I live on, as you can see. You are not yet dead, and when you are, you will not live again." I then moved the lever out again, putting me back in my original position behind him. I saw him quickly reach down and scoop up a large handful of sand in the direction of where I was standing seconds ago. As I expected, he fell on his face when he reached the position where I was supposed to be.

"You see? Even if you were to get close enough to touch me, it would do you no good. I am already dead to your world. I on the other hand, am very capable of killing you." I reached down and picked up the sheath for the dagger that he had thrown to the grown. I took several steps in his direction and threw it as hard as I could, hitting him in the chest. The sheath was made out of metal and was very solid. In and of itself it could be used as a weapon if the need arose. He grunted at the impact, and fell to his knees, writhing in pain. "I will take leave from you now because you have bested me. Should we meet again you may not be so blessed. Somehow, I will discover your ways and come looking for you."

I steeled myself and spat my last words to the high priest into the wind. "If you look for me, you will surely die a painful and terrible death, be warned!"

CHAPTER 32

BEWILDERED AND ASTONISHED

With that I thought of my kitchen and pushed in on the lever, tracking sand on my kitchen floor. I took off the cape and folded it and put it into my briefcase along with the ring and dagger. I sat the carry bag on the table and began to remove the other items I retrieved from the sarcophagus. One by one, I unwrapped them. The first one was a golden goblet; I inspected it carefully, looking at every detail. I saw nothing unusual about it. Next was crystal ball about the size of a large grapefruit and the pedestal that it sat on. I wasn't ready to figure out just what that was about just yet. The next two were scrolls. I sat them aside. The last item was a rolled up papyrus scroll and on the edge was printed in English: 'DR. RAZZ FREEMAN'. I became lightheaded for a second. I was stunned. I had just brought all this stuff back from a tomb that was from the time of Christ and it had a letter addressed to me? I unrolled the papyrus. It was truly a letter from Onias himself. I read it aloud.

Dr. Razz Freeman,

If you are reading this, it means that I have truly seen the future, as you will soon do. It also means that you have defeated the high priest, sorcerer and assassin Okto. You have done humanity a great deed. The scrolls will give you instruction on how to use the gifts I have left for you. I have seen that you are pure of heart, but are willing to fight for truth. I have provided for you in other ways to ensure you had the means to follow the clues to recover the treasures you now have. Your home truly belongs to you, for you are the true heir of it. The previous owner was your father's brother, adopted at birth, and otherwise hidden from the clan. The records of adoption are in Fairfield County.

Lastly, do not believe all that you see. Let your soul be your guide.

I sat stunned. The owner of this house was my uncle who had built this house and fortune for me? All this at once had drained me of strength. I sat back in my chair and shut my eyes, thinking that if I opened them it would all be a dream.

I reached for the scrolls and began to read the instructions. I had a feeling my adventures were just beginning.

The End (maybe)

RASPUTIN'S CLOAK OF DARKNESS
Continues in
BOOK TWO
Dr. Razz will be
Searching for answers about UFO's, Bigfoot and
The kidnapping of a US Senator and
The rescue of three aliens

Printed in Great Britain
by Amazon

61064583R00057